Dear Parents,

Welcome to the Scholastic Reader series. We have taken over 80 years of experience with teachers, parents, and children and put it into a program that is designed to match your child's interests and skills.

Level 1—Short sentences and stories made up of words kids can sound out using their phonics skills and words that are important to remember.

Level 2—Longer sentences and stories with words kids need to know and new "big" words that they will want to know.

Level 3—From sentences to paragraphs to longer stories, these books have large "chunks" of text and are made up of a rich vocabulary.

Level 4—First chapter books with more words and fewer pictures.

It is important that children learn to read well enough to succeed in school and beyond. Here are ideas for reading this book with your child:

- Look at the book together. Encourage your child to read the title and make a prediction about the story.
- Read the book together. Encourage your child to sound out words when appropriate. When your child struggles, you can help by providing the word.
- Encourage your child to retell the story. This is a great way to check for comprehension.
- Have your child take the fluency test on the last page to check progress.

Scholastic Readers are designed to support your child's efforts to learn how to read at every age and every stage. Enjoy helping your child learn to read and love to read.

—**Francie Alexander**
Chief Education Officer
Scholastic Education

Ms. Frizzle

Liz

Written by Eva Moore with consultation by Joanna Cole.

Illustrated by Carolyn Bracken.

Based on The Magic School Bus books written by Joanna Cole and illustrated by Bruce Degen.

The author and editor would like to thank Kristina Timmerman of the University of Minnesota Fisheries and Wildlife Department and Dave Garshelis of the Minnesota Department of Natural Resources for their expert advice in preparing this manuscript.

ISBN 0-439-56989-3

12 11 10   8/0 9/0 10/0

Designed by Peter Koblish

Printed in the U.S.A.
First printing, November 2003

The Magic School Bus® SLEEPS FOR THE WINTER

Arnold   Ralphie   Keesha   Phoebe   Carlos   Tim   Wanda   D. A.

Cartwheel BOOKS®

SCHOLASTIC INC.

New York   Toronto   London   Auckland   Sydney
Mexico City   New Delhi   Hong Kong   Buenos Aires

The real bear eats some nuts.
The bus-bear eats nuts, too.

**The bears sleep and sleep.
But we are not sleepy.
"Let's go outside,"
whispers the Friz.**

Two baby bears were born!
They are very small.
And they don't have fur yet.

AWAKE OR ASLEEP?
by Phoebe and Ralphie

Bears can wake up
for a short time.
But even then,
they're still half
asleep.

An animal that can
wake is called a
"light hibernator."

The visitors love our room.
They love Ms. Frizzle's dress, too!

Bear

Snake

Mice

Groundhogs

Toads

Frogs

Bats

Turtle

Z-Z-Z-Z

Fluency Fun

The words in each list below end in the same sounds.
Read the words in a list.
Read them again.
Read them faster.
Try to read all 15 words in one minute.

found	driving	another
round	getting	beaver
sound	growling	hunter
ground	skating	mother
around	sleeping	winter

Look for these words in the story.

animals	breathe	people
enough	hibernate	

Note to Parents:
According to *A Dictionary of Reading and Related Terms*, fluency is "the ability to read smoothly, easily, and readily with freedom from word-recognition problems." Fluency is necessary for good comprehension and enjoyable reading. The activities on this page include a speed drill and a sight-recognition drill. Speed drills build fluency because they help students rapidly recognize common syllables and spelling patterns in words, and they're fun! Sight-recognition drills help students smoothly and accurately recognize words. Practice these activities with your child to help him or her become a fluent reader.

—**Wiley Blevins,**
Reading Specialist